Whale Riding Weather

Whale Riding Weather

Bryden MacDonald

Talonbooks Vancouver 1994

Copyright © 1994 Bryden MacDonald

Published with the assistance of the Canada Council.

Talonbooks
201 - 1019 East Cordova
Vancouver, British Columbia
Canada V6A 1M8

Typeset in Galliard and printed and bound in Canada by Hignell
Printing Ltd.

First Printing: August 1994

Canadian Cataloguing in Publication Data

MacDonald, Bryden, 1960-
  Whale riding weather

  A play.
  ISBN 0-88922-353-X

  1. Title.
PS8575.D61W52 1994   C812'.54   C94-910663-1
PR9199.3.M32W52 1994

Dedicated
to the memory of my father
Dr. John Bryden MacDonald
who still
carries on with his support.

PRODUCTION CREDITS

Whale Riding Weather premiered at the Factory Theatre in Toronto, on October 31, 1991, with the following cast:

LYLE	Allan Gray
AUTO	Randy Hughson
JUDE	Patrick Galligan

DIRECTED BY Annie Kidder
DESIGNED BY John Ferguson
LIGHTING DESIGN BY Sholem Dolgoy
SOUND DESIGN BY David Akal Jaggs
STAGE MANAGER Judy Farthing

The Factory Theatre production was remounted in Toronto in November, 1992, with the same cast and crew, with the exception of Stage Manager, who was Paul Mark.

§

Halifax's Neptune Theatre production ran from 23 to 28 February, 1993, with the following cast and crew:

LYLE	Walter Borden
AUTO	Dennis Fitzgerald
JUDE	Kenneth Wilson-Harrington

DIRECTED BY Bryden MacDonald
DESIGNED BY Stephen Osler
LIGHTING DESIGN BY Brock Lumsden
STAGE MANAGER: Kimberley Hirtle

§

In Vancouver, Touchstone Theatre mounted a production of *Whale Riding Weather* at the Firehall Arts Centre from November 4 - 28, 1993. The same production had a hold-over run from December 16, 1993 to January 22, 1994, with the following cast and crew:

LYLE	Allan Gray
AUTO	Randy Hughson
JUDE	Joe-Norman Shaw

DIRECTED BY Roy Surette
DESIGNED BY David Roberts
LIGHTING DESIGN BY Kevin Lamotte
SOUND DESIGN BY Tippy Agogo and Douglas Macaulay
STAGE MANAGER: Sarah Martin

ACKNOWLEDGEMENTS

Thank you to my family—
and my friends
who are fortunately many
the Canada Council
and the wild wonderful
women at Factory Theatre
Jackie Maxwell
Dian English
and especially Annie Kidder
who along with
Allan Gray
Randy Hughson
and Patrick Galligan
were instrumental
in shaping this play
and to all the lives
and memories
that helped fuel it.

—BRYDEN MACDONALD

The huge blue bastard
was covered with old wounds
and deep gashes.
A steel harpoon claw still stuck in him
and he was blind in one eye.
He planed water
not like a little silver fish
in a Renaissance miniature
but like a real whale
that can smash and bruise the sea.

—Mark Helprin, *Winter's Tale*

A PLAY *for three men*
in eight scenes.

For pre-show and between
scenes — a collage of
inner-city sounds
mixed with the heavy
bass line of fruit disco
and crying cats.

§

The time is now
or later.
The action takes place
in the city of Toronto
over a two-day period
in a very small bachelor compartment
in a very old building
that was once quite elegant
that was once home to one family
but now
houses a number of compartments
ruled by an absentee landlord.

A glorious old tattered chaise longue
dominates the playing area.
This is where LYLE *sleeps.*

A bookcase partitions off the room.
Behind the partition but not visible
is a small cot.
This is where AUTO *sleeps.*

The room
full to capacity
with LYLE's *last possessions*
resembles a flea market.

In one cluttered frightening corner
is a make-shift pen of plywood
with hundreds of small air holes:
home to at least a dozen cats.
Their cries
resound periodically.

In the past
both LYLE *and* AUTO
attempted to create
and acknowledge
their own space
however
they have long ago
discontinued this practice
as the air is too stale and thick
to accommodate borders.

SCENE ONE

/early morning/

LYLE *is sprawled like a failed starlet*
on the chaise lounge
wrapped in soiled bed sheets.
He is forty-five
fifty
maybe sixty-five years old.
He is balding.
He is thin but going to flab.
There is a waxen
amphibious quality about him
and though the years have not been kind
he has sparkling
watery mischievously youthful
possibly borrowed eyes.
He wears bikini briefs.

LYLE *has surrounded himself*
with daily necessities
including a princess telephone
an ornate hand mirror
his ever-present bottle of sherry
and a crystal shot glass
so he rarely leaves
the security of the chaise.

AUTO *sits*
in an un cushioned straight-back chair
at a small table.
He rolls cigarettes
and chain smokes methodically.
There is a twenty-four
of warm canned American beer
on the floor beside him.

He drinks continuously.
He wears a pair of old
standard white briefs
the elasticized waist failing.
His hair is dry and knotted.
He is twenty-nine years old.
A frozen child.
A handsome frightened creature.

While LYLE speaks
AUTO does not acknowledge him
except where noted
he simply continues
to roll cigarettes and drink.

LYLE

I'm not bloodthirsty I'm efficient!

LYLE pours another sherry.

For Godsake—someone has to be.
Someone has to be on top of this transition period
this "new" limbo that's sending us spinning
sending us flying into this "new" madness
we so coyly refer to as a "new" age.
Someone has to be real for crissake.
You have to be real to survive the cocktail parties alone:
all of those drug-induced soliloquies
delivered by a relative of a relative of a somebody.
All of those debates
on "necessary assumption" and the "validity of shock."
Jesus Mary and Joseph
and the little mule too!
You can be trampled by an ego in a minute in this town.
Four Ace cards are never enough.
You need a stacked deck dear.

He downs his sherry
and pours another.

First Rule: never get drunk —
sober in a room full of plastered megalomaniacs
is the only way to go.
A soda with a twist. A cranberry juice.
Just smile and watch and disagree.
You can get away with never having to explain yourself
if you smile the right way and disagree.
Now granted
some of the more intelligent ones
might try to expose you
but not to worry dear —
there's nothing to expose
everyone knows what everyone else is up to anyway.
Oh they'll call you names
slut parasite starfucker
but the intelligent
are really not that difficult to keep in line.
It's like snakes and ladders dear —
looks tricky but it's really a snap.

There are however
far more snakes than ladders
and some quite venomous
but that type rarely work anyway.
It's the garter snakes you have to watch for
the North American breed
with the longitudinal stripes
that everyone is afraid of for no reason at all:
just snap your fingers in their face a few times
and they're completely stunned.

Another sherry.

And for crissake
don't expose too much talent too soon
even if it's only macramé you've mastered
remember
mediocrity rises.
Sometimes this can be quite a strain
but restrain yourself —
just swallow your pride
and touch your privates a lot.

A chuckle.
More sherry.

I used to say to a friend of mine —
I choose not to reveal her name.
If you remember anything I've taught you Auto
remember to be loyal to those who have been loyal to you.
At any rate
I used to say to my friend:
"Blank — it's just all too real
too real in the wrong sense of the word
for crissake
drop a tab of acid in that rig's campari."
And Blank would! The silly bitch did!
Everyone thought she was so sweet and goddamn innocent
but let me tell you
she did get some strange vicarious thrill
out of watching the pseudo-inspired flip out on drugs.
That little beaded clutch of hers was full of the stuff.
God bless her dear sweet bitter little heart —
she's in America now
in the Betty Ford wing with the rest of the girls.
But she'll be back again.
Front and centre
and bigger and better than ever.
Good Gawd —
could I tell stories. Plenty. Oh!

18

"There's plenty."
Wasn't she dreadful in that film?
And I told her. I had to. She's a dear friend.
Only university professors liked that film.
Good Gawd —
intellectuals —
maybe those crazed fundamentalists are right:
all intellectuals want to do is sleep with your children.

> *Silence.*

Auto?

> *LYLE raises his glass.*

Auuuutoooo?

> *AUTO looks to LYLE.*

This is just cranberry juice.

> *AUTO turns back*
> *to rolling cigarettes and drinking.*

And if you believe that —
I've got a small cock.

> *LYLE laughs*
> *downs his sherry*
> *and pours another.*

Oh I think intellectuals are kind of cute.
So paranoid.
Cast them a glance
with an expression on your face akin to that
when you get a whiff of off milk
and they flip

their day is ruined
because with impeccable timing
you can have them convinced
that they really didn't see anything at all.
It isn't cruel really.
More naughty.
Like turning a frog over on its back.
Now of course like anything
this too can be taken to extremes:
I knew children when I was growing up
who purchased tomato juice with their allowance
and spread it with a bit of salt
over unsuspecting frogs' bellies
and
well
in the sunlight the frogs would eventually explode.
Children can be obscene creatures.
There are some who should be prosecuted
but others who are rarely given credit when credit is due.
I was a very perceptive child
as I believe all children are
but we tend to lose it don't we
or disguise it
that's probably more apt
as we grow older.

Another sherry.

We spend so much time
wondering how far we can take it
when the answer is so obvious:
you take it as far as you possibly can —
and a little bit farther
if your Muses don't get too jealous.

Silence.

I suppose my Muses got too jealous —
is that what happened to me? No.
No I was destroyed. And it was no Muse.
I was destroyed because I trusted — completely! Hah!
Didn't I?
Didn't I Auto didn't I?
Auto?

> AUTO *looks to* LYLE.
> *Silence.*
> AUTO *turns back to drinking*
> *And rolling cigarettes.*

> LYLE *downs his sherry*
> *And pours another.*

> *Silence.*

Under Veronica's care
he's probably screaming "faggot" from car windows
and beating women by now.
Not that I was the ideal father image but —
he loved me. David loved me.
David loved his father
till that bitch poisoned him
till that cunt got her talons in him.
Yes.
Well.
Believing.
Believing in.
Believing in and.
Well.
Bang. Gone.
So easy.
Zip.

> *Silence.*

LYLE sips his sherry.
Silence.

Auto
you haven't brought anyone home in a long time Auto.
There must be some nice boys out there
boys who would consider it a privilege to be close to you.
No? Or are their senses all muted by fashion?
Well. There is someone. There is someone out there.
You are beautiful and brilliant and honest: lost qualities.
You just have to be patient.

Silence.

I'm only sick because of the torment she has caused me.
The anguish had no choice but to show itself physically.
But is she in jail where she belongs?
Is she locked up like she should be? No.

How can she live with herself?
I gave till I was empty.
I gave till I was dust till I was base:
a hologram for crissake. And then
when I am trying to claw my way out of the ashes
when I am trying to fill my world again — what?
I am forced to fight the very woman I helped keep alive.
Did I want it to be ugly? No.
I was simply trying to gain access to my son
but with every boy I ever winked at
or turned my head a second time to look at
sitting in the witness box — well —
Mary takes a nose dive doesn't she —
right out the proverbial fucking window.
I don't know how she avoids the guilt.
I don't know why she hasn't hung herself
or flung her godawful body
from the top of some architectural nightmare

22

which is all this city seems to produce:
hideous inhuman slabs of shit!

He downs his sherry.

And she covered all her tracks.
Dragging you into the picture too:
my little "concubine"
my little "catamite" — evil bitch!
I should have fought the cow —
should never have allowed her to "buy" me out.
Buy out.
Oh yes I got money didn't I.
Half. Didn't I.
The homes. The property.
Had I believed in myself more
I could have fought her.
But ultimately
what choice did I have?
humiliation and alienation WITH
or without money.
So while she sat there
cleaning her "glamour-length" nails
with an X-ACTO Knife
I sold my son. Oh there are monsters
there are monsters in this translucent world
don't ever doubt that Auto.

He pours another sherry
and sips it slowly.

How old is he now I wonder?
How old am I? Auto?
Auto
you haven't brought anyone home in a long time Auto.
There must be some nice boys out there
boys who would consider it a privilege to be close to you.

No? Or are their senses all muted by fashion?
Well. There is someone. There is someone out there.
You are beautiful and brilliant and honest: lost qualities.
You just have to be patient.

> AUTO *inhales a deep breath*
> *and exhales.*
> *He turns to* LYLE.

                              AUTO
Do you have any money?

> *Silence.*

                              LYLE
What?

                              AUTO
Do you have any money?

                              LYLE
Why?

                              AUTO
I want to go for a walk.

                              LYLE
You don't need money to walk.

                              AUTO
I might want to stop —
and buy something.

                              LYLE
I'm going to roast a duck for supper —
with baked pears.
If you're not going to be here I won't.

AUTO

I need a few bucks Lyle.

LYLE

Where are you going?

AUTO

For a walk.
I need a walk.
Just a walk.

LYLE

Will you be home if I roast a duck?

AUTO

You're not going to roast a duck Lyle.

LYLE

If you're not going to be here I won't.
There's no sense in my preparing —

AUTO

Do you need anything?

LYLE

Do I need anything?
Look at me —
what do you think?

AUTO

Do you want me to get you anything while I'm out?

LYLE

Where do you go?
Who do you go to?
How many more stories
are flaying around this city at my expense?

                    AUTO

Answer the question.

                    LYLE

What question?

                    Silence.
                    AUTO looks to LYLE.

                    LYLE

Will you get cat food?

                    AUTO

Yes.

                    LYLE

When they get to hungry
their magic wanes.
You must always remember that Auto.

                    AUTO

Where is it?

                    LYLE

Where is what?

                    Silence.
                    AUTO looks to LYLE.

                    LYLE

In the special drawer.

                    AUTO

WHICH special drawer?

LYLE

Remember that valiant oak desk
from my old atelier? Remember?

AUTO

Which. Special. Drawer.

LYLE

With the silver wear. With the linen napkins.
Under the linen napkins.

AUTO moves to the drawer.

LYLE

Remember when we were safe and we could travel?

*AUTO takes twenty dollars
from an overstuffed envelope
then returns the envelope to the drawer.*

AUTO

I'm just taking twenty.

LYLE

Are you getting thin?

Silence.

LYLE

I asked you a question!

AUTO

Don't bark at me.

LYLE

Don't! make! me bark!

They stare at each other.
Silence.
AUTO goes behind the partition.
Silence.

LYLE

Auto?
Auto something lovely happened the other day
and I neglected to tell you.

Another sherry.

LYLE

I was in a lounge.
A gentlemen's lounge — the name escapes me.
I was coming from a gruelling session with my lawyer
concerning that piece of land back east I'm interested in.
Veronica is dead set against it.
Veronica thinks we have far too much to keep up as it is.
But David will need a place for quiet.
And so will you.
To get out of the city.
To rest.
You get on fine with David.
I'm thinking maybe both of you could build on it some day.
But Veronica —
well Veronica thinks we —

He forgets
or he remembers.
Silence.

LYLE

It was a lovely little place.
Very quiet. Dimly lit.

I had been walking —
I had been visiting old friends and was quite thirsty
so I stopped in at this little lounge for a quick cocktail —
just one before I headed home.
At any rate
just as I was finishing my margarita and preparing to leave
the bartender arrived with another
and with a piece of paper — no
it was a matchbook
and written on that match book
in exquisite masculine scrawl:
"You are a very attractive young man
please join me — question mark"
delivered from a gentleman across the room.
But I didn't have time to join him.
I barely had time to finish the drink.
I could only thank him.
But what a lovely gesture.

> *AUTO re-enters.*
> *He is dressed*
> *in old blue jeans*
> *and an oversized hand-knit wool sweater*
> *his favourite sweater*
> *his oldest sweater*
> *possibly his only sweater.*
> *The colour is blood red: warm and safe.*
> *Also*
> *a pair of tattered Kodiak boots.*
>
> *They stare at each other a moment.*

LYLE

I don't want to be alone long.

AUTO

You won't be.

LYLE

What if they try to get me?

AUTO

If you're very quiet Lyle
they won't know you're here.

LYLE

They're mischievous bastards.
They always find me.

AUTO

I'll call and check on you.

LYLE

Auto —

AUTO

I know Lyle.
Three rings. Hang up. Phone back.

LYLE

It's a nuisance I know
but you understand
it's the only way to assure my safety.
If they were to find me in this condition
with not enough strength
to even attempt to defend myself —

AUTO

Just watch television for awhile.

LYLE

Television!
I'd rather be set on fire.

> *AUTO produces a book of matches*
> *from his back pocket.*

                              AUTO

Matches?

                    They stare at each other a moment.
                    AUTO almost laughs.
                    LYLE is not impressed.

                              AUTO

Sorry.

                    AUTO puts the matches back in his pocket
                    moves to his table
                    fills a plastic cigarette case with cigarettes
                    and puts it in his pocket.

                              LYLE

Do I have more Sherry?

                              AUTO

Two bottles.

                              LYLE

Did you take your pill?

                              AUTO

I have them if I need one.

                              LYLE

We could play Scrabble today.

                              AUTO

I won't be long.

                              LYLE

Comb your hair.

                    AUTO exits the compartment
                    closing the door behind him.

                              LYLE

Auto?!

                              AUTO

Yes!
It's locked!

          Blackout.

SCENE TWO

/late afternoon/

                    LYLE is huddled on the chaise
                    wide awake
                    clutching his glass of sherry
                    staring longingly
                    into the ornate hand mirror
                    singing softly to himself:

                              LYLE

I know I stand in line
until you think you have the time
to spend an evening with me.
And if we go some place to dance
I know that there's a chance
you won't be leaving with me.
Then afterwards we drop into
a quiet little place and have a drink or two
and then I go and spoil it all
by saying something stupid
like I loooove you.
I know I stand in line
until you think you have the —

The telephone begins to ring.
LYLE stops singing abruptly
and acknowledges the ringing gingerly.

After the third ring
the ringing stops
and LYLE almost cries from relief.

After a moment
the phone begins to ring again.
LYLE grabs the receiver
before the first ring is finished.

Auto I've been having a terrible day.
I felt the last five beats of my heart.
Each beat lasting an eternity.
I've been dead since noon.

Auto are you there?
Listen carefully Auto —
this should all be documented.

LYLE pours a sherry.

During the first beat
I begin accepting apologies from everyone —
even strangers. And Veronica too —
I actually allow her to apologize
and then surprise myself even more
by pardoning her.
And the world is like a wave
like a great blue wave spinning round me like a wind
and then
during the second beat
I am loving a boy
a beautiful cowboy boy
and he doesn't want me to pay him

33

he only wants my love
and he says:
"I would very much like to see you again"
but I know I only have three beats left
so I have to decline.

And then —
Auto the third beat is so beautiful.
I'm worried and lazy and morose
but the third beat
in itself
is beautiful.
Beautifully timed. Musical. Intricate.
It's the middle beat
so it's the prettiest of the five
but even so
I find myself
valiantly giving my permission
to be belittled in public
and at the end
hah!
I'm just a poet.
Imagine. So simple.
But the cats were there.
The cats are with me my cats my witches
all through it all
and that amazes my audience
that I have such a large following of cats
but no people on my side.
And I wallow
mercilessly indulging myself.
I am such a wonderful martyr during this third beat Auto
and I'm wishing you could see me:
such a hungry old cow
bowing long after the applause.
But then
the fourth beat sneaks up like a rapist:

a pedantic old fool from some glorified school of shit —
a crusty overrated plebeian
and I am a queen at this point Auto
a fading dying starlet cast at my own feet
walking
knowing there are others following
and my body is in bloom
but I'm not singing —
I wish I was but I'm not.
They won't let me sing: amateurs!
And of course I'm on fire —
burning
praising the arsonist. And then the fifth beat
the fourth and the fifth are very closely connected.
But I know the fifth is the fifth
because no one is watching me anymore.
There is just me —
burning for my own entertainment.
And I die.
I die like I always knew I would die —
alone.
But teased first —
teased into believing by the four beats before
that it just might possibly
be a memorable death.

A deep breath.

What an enormous day Auto —
from Diva to death
in five quick beats.
What was that?

Auto what was that sound? that click?

There was a click Auto.
There was a sound.

The miserable bastards.
The miserable bastards have tapped this line.
The miserable fucking cowards have

> *He begins banging
> the receiver on the table.*

tapped! this! line!

> *The banging stops.
> Silence.
> LYLE brings the receiver to his ear.*

Auto?

Auto don't say another word Auto
just hang up the phone and run —
run as fast as you can.

Auto?

Auto are you there?

> *Blackout.*

SCENE THREE

/late evening/

> *A lamp by the chaise
> sheds the only light in the room
> illuminating the sheet-covered lump
> that is LYLE's sleeping body.*
>
> *A key in the door.*

36

The door opens
and AUTO *enters*
followed by JUDE.

JUDE doesn't drink continuously
as does AUTO
so his drunkenness is more apparent.

JUDE is a playful charming chatty drunk.
He wears tight faded black jeans
with fashionable rips
in the knees
the ass and around the crotch
now patched
with splashes of deep colour.
A billowing white
ruffle-down-the-chest shirt.
A black leather belt
with a large silver buckle.
A black frock coat
and Doc Martin boots.
He is clean shaven.
His hair is cropped short and uneven
blue-black
iridescent like a crow's wing.

He wears an old flash bulb camera
in its case
around his neck.
He is one year younger than AUTO.
He exudes a reluctant confidence.
He is horny.

As they enter
the cats are crying
and JUDE *is rambling.*

JUDE

I'm serious man
some fucked up bastards
strangled the swans.
Heard it on the news.
Six swans with broken necks
scattered all over the park.
Some bag lady found thum. She flipped out.
She usta feed thum right —
so she flipped out
and stabbed a cop with a broken wine bottle.
Wild. Who'd wanna strangle a swan? Fuck.
Prob'ly some poor little rich kids from the burbs
actin out some ah —
inferior satanic ritual or somethin right.
Poor ole Satan eh —
he's takin the rap for a lot a sick minds these days.

AUTO turns on a lamp
illuminating the pen.

AUTO

Jesus Christ I forgot cat food.

JUDE moves to the pen
and peers in.

JUDE

Fuck.
How many in there?

AUTO

Too many.

JUDE

How many?

                    AUTO

They belong to Lyle
This is his place.

                    JUDE

What? he collects thum?

                    AUTO

They protect him.

                    JUDE

Oh yeah?
They ever get out?

                    AUTO

No.

                    JUDE

You don't like cats?

                    AUTO

One
maybe two at a time.

                    JUDE

Yeah.
Funny thing cats.
Pretty demanding eh.
Always think you're playin with thum.
Even if ya kick thum or set thum on fire
they still think you're playin with thum.

          An awkward laugh from JUDE.
          Silence.

                    JUDE

They must be fixed eh.

                    AUTO
No.

                    JUDE
Oh.

          An awkward silence.

                    JUDE
They all have names?

                    AUTO
Hyphenated names.

          An awkward laugh from JUDE.

                    JUDE
Must get pretty crazy in there sometimes.

                    AUTO
Anyway this is it.
I warned you
it's not much.

               *JUDE moves to AUTO and embraces his
               waist.*

                    JUDE
Long as there's a bed.

               *JUDE fondles AUTO's ass and kisses him.
               AUTO neither acknowledges nor rejects
               this.*

                    JUDE
So —
what did ya say ya do again?

                              AUTO
I didn't.
I don't do anything.

                    AUTO moves to LYLE.

                              AUTO
There's beer on the floor by that table.

                              JUDE
Um.
Thanks.

                    JUDE grabs a beer.

Too many more a these
I'll prob'ly be pretty useless to ya —
but I doubt that.

                         *JUDE laughs to himself
                         and cracks the beer.*

                              AUTO
Lyle?

                              JUDE
Fuck. Oh wow. Hi pal.
You the cat man?

                    LYLE mumbles incoherently.

Didn't even see him. The cat man?

                         *AUTO drums his fingers
                         gently on LYLE's table.
                         LYLE awakens abruptly with a gasp.*

LYLE

Is it October?!

AUTO

There's company.

LYLE

Company? we have company? but look at me?! Who?
A boyfriend?
I dreamed you met someone — I think.
I think I did.
I didn't cook because you didn't come home.
Who's that?

> AUTO *doesn't respond.*
> *He moves to his table*
> *and begins to roll cigarettes and drink.*
> *Silence.*

JUDE

Ah. Hi. Lyle?
Sorry ta wake ya man — didn't see ya there.
Jude.

LYLE

Jude?

JUDE

Jude. J - U - D - E.

LYLE

Well well my my — how appropriate —
the patron saint of hopeless causes
right here in this very room.

JUDE

Um.
My mom didn't know that when she named me.

42

LYLE

I know everything there is to know about two things —
romance and the Bible.
A Caaaaaaaaaatholic. All of us —
hopeless guilt-ridden romantics.

JUDE

Oh yeah?

JUDE glances to AUTO
who appears oblivious.

LYLE

Well well my my —
Auto rarely entertains
soooooo
I suppose I should make myself scarce.
Shall I take the guest room Auto?
It's just beyond our library Jude.

JUDE

Ah —
cool.

LYLE

Shall I Auto?
Shall I take the guest room Auto?

AUTO

Whatever you like Lyle.

LYLE

Auto and I have a very open relationship.
Auto?
Auto might I have one small cocktail before I retire?
Auto and I try to be as accommodating as possible
when a situation like this arises.
That's a lovely blouse.

JUDE

Um.
Thanks.

LYLE

Auto may I have one more small cocktail?
just a tiny one before I retire?
Auto?

AUTO

Fill your boots Lyle.

LYLE

Cocktail?

JUDE

Got one thanks.

LYLE pours a sherry.

LYLE

I was sleeping Auto.
I believe I was actually sleeping.
I have a bit of a sleeping disorder Jude — I don't.

JUDE

That's a drag.

*JUDE glances at AUTO
who continues to roll cigarettes and drink.*

LYLE

Horrific.
But after charting my own demise this afternoon
I do believe I was actually sleeping.
Was it this afternoon?
I kept poor Auto on the phone forever.

Did you get away without being seen baby?
Did they see you?
Auto?

AUTO

No.

JUDE

Who?

LYLE

Bastards!
Nazi! bastards!

LYLE *downs his sherry.*

LYLE

Excuse me — Jude?

JUDE

Yeah. Jude.

LYLE

I'm afraid I'll have to see some identification.

JUDE

Pardon?

AUTO

Lyle.

LYLE

Dear?

AUTO

Did you sleep?

45

Yes. Oh yes —
and God knows I deserved a good sleep.
I had a horrific day Jude.
May you never experience a day
as long as you live Jude
may you never experience a day
like the day I had today.
I died. I died a pauper's death.
I won't go into detail —
no need to open Pandora's box twice in the same day.
Well —
I'm going to have a closer look at you.
I'm actually going to get up.

> *LYLE waddles when he walks.*
> *This waddle*
> *at one time*
> *may have been an attractive mince*
> *but now*
> *it is just a waddle.*

LYLE

Please excuse my appearance —
everything's at the laundry.
I've been very busy.
A busy bee.

> *LYLE stands close to JUDE*
> *frightened*
> *almost childlike*
> *but LYLE does not touch JUDE.*
> *JUDE is not uncomfortable.*

Oh Auto he's lovely.
But you are the lucky one Jude —
having my Auto choose you.
Isn't my Auto beautiful?

JUDE

No argument there.

AUTO remains oblivious.

LYLE

Auto's very old.
He's been told by numerous psychics
that this is his last life.

JUDE

Oh yeah?

LYLE

Yes. Oh yes —
his palms are very full —
that's a sure sign.
And he's a painter — did he tell you that?
but he doesn't paint nearly as much as he should.
And if that's not enough
he writes poetry and plays piano.
We had a piano when we summered in Venice.
This place —
this place is only temporary.
It's become increasingly difficult
to find adequate housing in this city don't you find?
Oh! You're a photographer.

JUDE

I just take pictures.

LYLE

Of what?

JUDE

Things.
Things I like.

LYLE

May I?

JUDE

Sure.

> *Without removing the camera*
> *from* JUDE's *neck*
> LYLE *holds it in his palms for a moment*
> *as if it was an injured sparrow*
> *and then lets it rest gently*
> *on* JUDE's *chest.*
> *They smile.*

LYLE

You have gentle eyes.

JUDE

Thank you.

LYLE

Let me see your bum.

JUDE

What?

> LYLE *makes a "turn around" gesture.*
> JUDE *laughs and complies*
> *lifting his jacket.*
> LYLE *gazes at* JUDE's *ass.*

LYLE

Oh Auto he is lovely.

> AUTO *glances.* JUDE *catches the glance*
> *and extends his tongue to* AUTO.

*LYLE does not see this exchange.
AUTO turns back to drinking
and rolling cigarettes.*

LYLE

But I dare not touch.

*JUDE drops his jacket back in place
and turns to LYLE.*

JUDE

Free show's over.

LYLE

Oh!
Let me show you something Jude.

*LYLE moves to the cabinet
to get his photo album.
JUDE looks to AUTO.
AUTO remains oblivious.*

LYLE

It's a photo of my Aunt Sig.
My Aunt Sig was a very extreme very eccentric thing.
An angel. A witch.
She had a fear of fires —
believed she was burned at the stake in another life
and probably was if she said so.
She was the first to recognize Auto's genius.
Isn't that right Auto?
She's dead now — bless her.
Gawd how she spoiled me.
She was the only woman I could tolerate.
Most women make me nauseous —
lizards most are.

                    AUTO
Lyle.

                    LYLE
Sluts. Cunts.

                    AUTO
Lyle.

                    LYLE
If you ever had to —

                    AUTO
Stop.

            Silence.

                    LYLE
I want to show Jude my photograph.

                    AUTO
Later.

            Silence.

                    LYLE
Yes. Later. Well —
very nice to meet you Jude.
I'm sure you'll enjoy my chaise.
I've bedded many lovers there
both foreign and common
in exquisite discomfort.
Good night.

                    JUDE
Night night.

LYLE

Good night Auto.

AUTO

Sleep well Lyle.

LYLE moves reluctantly
behind the partition.
Silence.
JUDE whispers:

JUDE

What? did his mother torture him?

AUTO

He gets confused.

JUDE

Are you maybe bein generous?

AUTO

He gets confused.

JUDE

Can he hear us?

AUTO

He has to see you to really hear you.

JUDE

Oh yeah? He's not far away.

AUTO

You're just one more voice to him —
let's just leave it at that.

JUDE

No problem.

AUTO

This was a mistake.
I think you should go.

JUDE

So —

JUDE pulls a string of condoms
from his back pocket
and moves to the chaise.

JUDE

We sleep here?

JUDE unlaces his boots
and kicks them off.

JUDE

What are ya doin tomorrow?
I'm goin to this brunch thing at my friend's place —
Carrie and Rue —
couple a urban-dyke-witches I been hangin out with.
I can bring someone.
Tomorrow's first day of the full moon —
they'll be howlin.

AUTO

I don't think so.

JUDE

Why?

AUTO

Jude —

52

                    JUDE
Don't decide now.

                    AUTO
It's been decided.

          JUDE removes his jacket
          and unbuttons his shirt.

                    JUDE
Think about it.
But think about me first.

          JUDE unbuckles his belt
          unbuttons the top button of his jeans
          and flops on the chaise.

                    JUDE
Fuckin Cleopatra man.

          AUTO continues to roll cigarettes
          and drink.

          Silence.

          AUTO looks to JUDE.
          JUDE winks and grins.
          AUTO turns back to rolling cigarettes
          And drinking.

                    AUTO
It's late.

          JUDE bursts into spontaneous song
          with an Elvis twist and twang:

                    53

JUDE

It's late.
And it's great that it's late.
And it's fate
that it's great that it's late.
I gotta date.
Can't fuckin wait.
Thank God I'm not straight.
Kiss me Kate.
Thang you
thang you very much.

AUTO almost smiles.

AUTO

Jude —

JUDE

I'm glad we finally met.

AUTO

Finally?

JUDE

You know what I mean.

AUTO

I do?

JUDE

You do.
Yes you do.
Somethin happened when I caught your eye.
You didn't break the stare.
You let me take your picture.
I felt a spark.
You trembled.
You were lookin for me in that barroom.

                    AUTO

Finished?

                    JUDE

You got a light around you.
Not much colour.
Just a glow.
But it's there.

                    AUTO

You're cute Jude —
and you're drunk.

                    JUDE

It's not cuz I'm drunk.
I been drunk a lot.
I been around the block —
more than twice.
Done the bars. Lots. Too much.
And I know when somethin happens.
And somethin happened.
Somethin clicked.

                    AUTO

How old are you?

                    JUDE

I don't lie.
I usta lie a lot.
I don't lie anymore.
I think it's best to just um — say it.
What the fuck —
let thum laugh right?

                    AUTO

I go to that bar
once or twice a week
looking for nothing
but quiet.

                    JUDE

Quiet?

                    AUTO

Quiet.
That's all I go out to pick up.

                    JUDE

I'm a lot of things
but I'm not fuckin quiet.

                    AUTO

Jude.

                    JUDE

You're lyin.

                    AUTO

Jude.

              JUDE spits out
              a slurring Brando godfather:

                    JUDE

Gimme a fuckin break man
I'm spread out here
like a buffet dinner
the least ya can do
is pour honey on my tits
or suck my toes.

              AUTO almost smiles.

                    AUTO

I haven't been with anyone in a very long time.

                    JUDE

Then get over here.

                    56

*AUTO cracks a beer
and lights a cigarette.*

JUDE

Why did you take me home?

AUTO

You begged me to.

JUDE

Fuck off —
you wanted me to beg.

Silence.

JUDE

You don't talk a lot.

Silence.

JUDE

You got a beautiful voice.

AUTO

No more compliments are necessary.

Silence.

JUDE

Come lay on top of me.

Silence.

AUTO

Jude. I'm sorry.
I shouldn't have —

                              JUDE
Don't think about it anymore
just do it.

                    Silence.
                    All still.

                    Then
                    AUTO puts his cigarette out
                    takes one more slug of beer
                    and moves slowly
                    to stand in front of JUDE.

                    Silence.

                              AUTO
You come from a good home don't you.

                              JUDE
I used to.
I guess.

                              AUTO
You're lucky.

                              JUDE
Take your sweater off.

                              AUTO
I'm a lousy lay.

                              JUDE
Take your sweater off.

                    All still.
                    Then
                    AUTO takes his sweater off.

                    58

JUDE

Smile.

AUTO

I am.

> *All still.*
> *JUDE is on his knees.*
> *JUDE rest his cheek against AUTO's crotch.*
> *And just as he*
> *is unbuttoning AUTO's pants*
> *LYLE enters with his photo album.*

LYLE

Excuse me boys —
did you get cat food Auto?

JUDE

When it rains it pours.

AUTO

No Lyle.
I forgot.

> *JUDE kisses AUTO's ass.*
> *AUTO steps away*
> *so JUDE is just out of reach*
> *and buttons up his pants.*

AUTO

I'm sorry.

JUDE

What's shakin Lyle?

LYLE

My insides darling.

                              AUTO
I'll get it tomorrow.

                              LYLE
It's the only little thing I asked you to do.

                              AUTO
Tomorrow Lyle.

                              LYLE
Fine dear
but if your friend doesn't mind
I think I should be allowed to stay up awhile longer.
Don't you think that's fair?

                              AUTO
Ask my friend.

                    AUTO goes back to his table
                    and continues to roll cigarettes
                    and drink.

                              LYLE
Do you mind Jude?

                              JUDE
No man. Fine. Your place.

                              AUTO
Just white lies?

                    JUDE smiles.
                    LYLE speaks to his cats.

                              LYLE
Num nums tomorrow babies.

Behind LYLE's back
JUDE gyrates
and feels himself for AUTO.
LYLE turns to the guys
and JUDE stops abruptly.
AUTO almost smiles.

LYLE

Well
I'm so glad you brought someone home Auto.
My Auto's been very testy lately.
I want you to be good to him Jude.

JUDE

Believe me —
I'm doin my best here Lyle.

AUTO almost smiles.

LYLE

Let me show you my crazy Aunt.

LYLE sits by JUDE
and opens the photo album.

LYLE

She was the youngest of nine.
The only girl.
I'm fairly certain she was an old Gertrude.

JUDE

Oh yeah?

JUDE looks to AUTO
who continues to roll cigarettes
and drink.

LYLE

You know dear —
women play a very important role in my life.
I feel much closer to women than I do men.
A man can please me physically
but that's all.
You know?

JUDE

Ah —
I suppose.

LYLE

I find the concept of women far more appealing.

JUDE

Concept?

LYLE

Yes dear —
the state of.

JUDE

Okay.

JUDE looks to AUTO
who appears oblivious.

LYLE

Sig loved Auto.
She was ancient when they first met.
Auto tell Jude about the first time you met Aunt Sig.

AUTO

I'm tired Lyle.

JUDE

Gettin a bit yawny here myself Lyle.

LYLE

How long have I been up?

AUTO

Long.

LYLE

Oh. Well —
will you be here tomorrow Jude?

JUDE

Yep.

> AUTO *looks to* JUDE.
> JUDE *winks at* AUTO.
> AUTO *turns back*
> *to drinking*
> *and rolling cigarettes.*

LYLE

I'll make croissant.
I always make croissant in the morning.
I keep the dough frozen
so it just takes minutes.

JUDE

Sounds great.

LYLE

But now —
to bed.
I'm jealous but I'll go to bed.
You're such a nice boy Jude.
So many little tarts running around these days.
Auto's a brilliant painter you know.
Show Jude your work Auto.

AUTO

Some other time Lyle.

                                LYLE

Did you take your pill?

                                AUTO

I didn't need it.

                                LYLE

Well that's good.
That's very good.
Okay —
I'm off to bed. Night night.
Don't sleep tight.

                                JUDE

Night Lyle.

                                LYLE

Good night dear.
Good night Auto.

                                AUTO

Good night Lyle.

                                LYLE

It's so nice to have company.

                    LYLE goes behind the partition.

                                JUDE

Wow.
He's wild.
He's somethin else.
How much of what he says is true?

                    Silence.
                    AUTO rolls cigarettes
                    and drinks beer.

                                64

Silence.
JUDE moves to AUTO
and offers his hand.

Silence.
All still.

AUTO touches JUDE's hand
recoils
then takes his hand.
JUDE leads auto to the chaise.
They sit.
JUDE begins to rub AUTO's neck.

JUDE

It's concrete.
Bend.

AUTO bends his head forward
and JUDE continues to rub.

JUDE

Why do you take pills?

AUTO

Sometimes I panic.

JUDE

Why?

AUTO

If you don't know
it can't be explained.

JUDE kisses AUTO's neck.

JUDE

You won't panic with me.

65

                    AUTO
Don't be so sure.

                    JUDE
And what Auto
automatic autopilot autograph
is that supposed to mean?

                    AUTO
Exactly what I said.

                Silence.
                JUDE continues to rub.

                    JUDE
I saw you in a dream.

                AUTO recoils from the massage.

                    JUDE
Relax.

                JUDE continues to rub AUTO's neck.

Yeah I saw you in a dream.
I'm sittin in my grandmother's kitchen.
I'm drinkin tea
and the worst thing is happenin:
I'm completely obsessed with how others look at me.
I'm sitting in my grandmother's kitchen
cuz it's the last place I have to go
and I'm completely obsessed with how others look at me.
The only safe place left
and I don't even feel safe there
and that's really weird
cuz I always felt safe in that kitchen.
Then I hear a rumble.

It's a train —
far away like poundin in my ears
and I know it's gonna stop in the kitchen.
I know it's comin for me.
I know it's gonna stop in the kitchen
and there's nothin I can do.
And then it arrives.
Smash.
Right through the wall.
It's an old locomotive
and it's covered with lilacs
because it came through my grandmother's backyard
right through her lilac bushes
and right through the kitchen wall.
And there's nothin I can do.
Hundreds of cars screamin through my grandmother's kitchen
and I can't do a fuckin thing.
Then finally after forever —
it stops.
And you walk out of the last car.

> *JUDE stops the massage.*
> *An awkward silence.*
> *Then:*

JUDE

The morning after that dream
my eyes changed colour.

> *Silence.*

I don't know where I come from
so I can't go back.

> *Silence.*
> *JUDE rests his head*
> *on AUTO's back.*

JUDE

Please don't laugh at me.
Do anything
but please don't laugh at me.

AUTO

That's asking a lot.

Silence.

JUDE

What would you do
if I said
I was only on this planet for you
and I'd be content
just to watch you sleep?

AUTO

I'd call the fucking cops.

JUDE smiles.

JUDE

I won't say that then.

AUTO

Wise choice.

Shy smiles.
Silence.
All still.

Then
slowly
AUTO's fingers
make their way to JUDE's face
to JUDE's mouth:
the blind reading.

LYLE appears from behind the partition.
He watches AUTO and JUDE for a
moment
and then
retires almost gracefully
behind the partition.

AUTO releases
a buried sound of pleasure
and slowly
very timidly
they begin to make love
as the lights fade to

Blackout.

SCENE FOUR

/early morning/

The sun is threatening to rise.
JUDE is sleeping on the chaise
his naked body
braided in the sheet
like a half-opened present.

AUTO
in his underwear
is rolling cigarettes
and drinking beer at his table.

Pause on this scene.

LYLE enters
from behind the partition.

AUTO doesn't see him.
LYLE gazes at JUDE.

Pause on this scene.

                    LYLE
Auto?

AUTO continues to drink
and roll cigarettes.

                    LYLE
Auto?

AUTO looks to LYLE.

                    LYLE
May I?

Silence.

Please?

AUTO turns back to drinking
And rolling cigarettes.

LYLE gazes at JUDE's sleeping body
and then
LYLE waddles slowly
frightened
toward JUDE.

LYLE kneels by JUDE.
AUTO looks to JUDE and LYLE
And then returns to drinking
And rolling cigarettes.

Pause on this scene.

Then
ever so gently
LYLE runs his hands
through JUDE's hair
and down and around
the length of his body.
JUDE at first
still sleeping
responds favourably
but then upon waking
and realizing the situation
he recoils abruptly.

Silence.

LYLE
For an instant you thought I was beautiful.

JUDE is staring at AUTO.
AUTO continues to drink
and roll cigarettes.
LYLE lowers his head.
Then
AUTO turns to JUDE and LYLE.
LYLE looks to AUTO.
AUTO turns back to drinking
and rolling cigarettes.
LYLE goes back behind the partition.

An awkward silence.

JUDE
Why did you let him do that?

Silence.

Auto why did you let him do that?

                              AUTO

Do what?

                              JUDE

Fuck off.
You held me so tight last night
I could barely breathe.

                              AUTO

You must have been dreaming again.

            Silence.

                              JUDE

Auto?

                              AUTO

You should leave now Jude.

                              JUDE

Auto —

                              AUTO

Please.
Now.

            AUTO guzzles his beer
            opens another
            and continues rolling cigarettes.

            A long hollow silence
            as a buried memory begins to fill JUDE.
            When he finally speaks
            it is with caution
            but conviction
            though he is unable to look at AUTO.

JUDE

Once.
A while ago.
It was a while ago.
I was even crazier than I am now.
This guy comes in the bar where I usta drink.
He starts passin out those key chains
with "I'm deaf" written on thum — lookin for money.
He pokes one in someone's face
and they say no.
Someone else's face. They say no.
Then he pokes one in my face
and I say no.
Then in someone else's face
and they say no.
Then in my face again.
This time he looks right inta me and —
he had dolphin eyes
big wide watery dolphin eyes:
ships coulda gone down in those eyes.
And he had nice hands.
Strong wrists.
Long fingers.
But I say no again and he —
he started sprayin
splashin
sprinklin those fingers in my face
those dolphin eyes wild and frightened
talkin at me with his hands
and I screamed
I screamed at him
"No! Go!"
Everyone in the bar was lookin and —
and he was lookin at me like —
I turned my head away.
He left.

Very contained
AUTO begins to panic.

JUDE

And I felt —
I felt somethin new somethin
somethin brand new and scary.
I didn't understand it at the time I
I didn't know what it meant at the time but
but I know now that
that when he left
and I almost ran after him but I didn't —
when
when he left
a chunk of me left with him.

Silence.
JUDE is able
to look at AUTO now.

JUDE

Auto so many people
so many people been livin together for years
but they got no idea who they're lookin at everyday.
None. No fuckin idea at all. It's true.
So maybe there's nowhere else for us to look Auto
except to each other.

Silence.

Auto how desperate do I have to sound?
There is no where else for us to look Auto.
We could stop.
We can stop.

AUTO

Get out.
Now.
Go.

74

Silence.
JUDE bolts from the chaise
searches for his underwear
crisp white briefs
and puts them on.
Then:

JUDE

Whether it means anything to you or not
I never followed my gut this far before.
Closest I ever came
was driving a van from a florist's shop
through an asshole's living room window
but that's another story.
I never gone this far before.

AUTO

Jude.

JUDE

No. Wait.

AUTO begins to hyperventilate.

JUDE

At least I did it.
At least I made the decision.
At least I made the decision to follow it up.
Gimme credit for that you fuckin asshole.
At least gimme credit for goin for it.
Hope ya enjoyed the ass.
It's the best you ever had
and the best you'll ever —

AUTO is obviously not well.

JUDE

What the fuck is wrong?

                          AUTO
There's a bottle of pills —

                    JUDE is already looking.
                    AUTO's breathing
                    is getting more irregular.

                          JUDE
Where?

                          AUTO
Pants pocket.

                          JUDE
Pants pocket pants pocket pants pocket
pants pants pants
where's your fuckin pants?
I don't remember that part.
I took thum off
no I chewed thum off.
Where's your fuckin pants? did I eat your fuckin pants?
D'ya blow-up d'ya need it right away? what's the story?
Where's! your fuckin pants?!

                    JUDE finds a pair of pants.

                          JUDE
They're mine.

                    He throws them aside
                    and continues to search.

                          JUDE
Don't die
just don't fuckin die.
Fuck!

JUDE finds AUTO's pants.

JUDE

Okay!

JUDE is digging through the pockets.

Okay okay okay.

JUDE finds the pills
opens them
and gives them to AUTO.
AUTO pops two
and guzzles some beer.

JUDE

Okay?
Okay?

An uncomfortable silence.
AUTO is doubled over
breathing heavily.
JUDE watches him carefully.

JUDE

Okay?

JUDE strokes AUTO's hair.

It's okay.

An uncomfortable silence.
JUDE begins to rub AUTO's neck
and kisses him gently.

It's okay.

An uncomfortable silence.
And then
When JUDE senses AUTO's return.

JUDE

Leave.

AUTO takes an enormous breath
and exhales.

AUTO

I can't.

JUDE

Why?

AUTO

I don't want to.

JUDE

Can't
don't want to
what?

AUTO recoils from the massage.

JUDE

There are people who can help him.

AUTO

He doesn't want help.
Just move away from me please just —
just give me more room.

JUDE complies.

JUDE

Why does he have so much control?

                    AUTO
No one has control here.

                    JUDE
Do you love him?

                    AUTO
He saved me.

          A sad chuckle from AUTO.

That man.
Saved me.

          *An awkward spurt of laughter from AUTO
          then silence.*

                    JUDE
He's dying.

                    AUTO
Tell me something I don't know.

                    JUDE
So are you.

                    AUTO
Try again.

                    JUDE
This room is killing you Auto.

                    AUTO
"This room is killing you Auto" what! What?!

          *AUTO bolts from his chair
          and grabs JUDE by the face
          almost lifting him from the floor.*

                    79

AUTO

What all of a sudden huh? What?!
I said get the fuck out of here didn't I?!

Hold this image.

Then
JUDE
fearless
opens his mouth.

Hold this image.

Then
AUTO relaxes his grip
and moves in to kiss JUDE.

LYLE enters.

LYLE

Well well well —

The kiss breaks
but AUTO and JUDE
remain gazing at each other.

LYLE

I thought I heard someone else out here.
Auto how could you?
this place is a mess.
Didn't we agree to check with each other
before we had company?
Really —
this is no way to entertain.

Silence.

Auto where are your manners?
Who is this young man?

*AUTO responds
without taking his eyes from JUDE.*

AUTO

This is Jude.

LYLE

Jude?

AUTO

Yes.
Jude.

Silence.

LYLE

Jude.

*LYLE goes back
behind the partition.*

JUDE

Thank you.

*AUTO runs his hands
through JUDE's hair.*

Blackout.

SCENE FIVE

/later morning/

> *JUDE stretched out on his back*
> *on the chaise.*
> *AUTO on top of JUDE*
> *licking JUDE's nipple.*

JUDE

I was in jail.

> *The licking stops.*

AUTO

What?

JUDE

I was in jail.

AUTO

Great.
What were you in for?
Being too cute?

JUDE

For lovin someone too much.
It was his living room I drove through.

AUTO

Lucky I'm two floors up.

JUDE

I don't love you too much.
I love you just enough.

> *Silence.*

                    AUTO
Did you strangle the swans?

                    JUDE
No.
Never.

                    AUTO
I dream of the hunt sometimes.
The kill.

                    JUDE
That's normal.

                    AUTO
Even when it's yourself you're hunting?
Yourself you're killing?

                    JUDE
Better than those dreams
when you're falling.

              Blackout.

SCENE SIX

/early afternoon/

              AUTO and JUDE
              are wrapped in an intricate knot
              of arms and legs on the chaise.

              Silence.

                            AUTO
Remembering.
Remembering is —

        Silence.

                            AUTO
By the time I was twelve years old
I had read everything.
Everything.
Didn't retain a fucking thing.
My parents wanted me to be gifted you see.
But I wasn't.
I'm not.

                            JUDE
I was gifted.
But I stopped.

        AUTO looks to JUDE.

                            JUDE
Go ahead — ask me somethin:
numbers especially.

                            AUTO
So —
you're a genius now?

                            JUDE
Yeah.

                            AUTO
Oh.

                            JUDE
Ask me somethin if ya want.
Numbers especially.

No big deal.
Quit school. Tired of performing.
I sew now.
Put patches on things.
And I do my friends taxes.
Need your taxes done?

                    AUTO
I don't make money.

                    JUDE
I could still get ya somethin back.

                    AUTO
Where the fuck did you come from?

                    JUDE
Keep talkin. Talk more.

                    AUTO
Talk more.

                    JUDE
Talk more.

                    AUTO
Um —

          JUDE kisses AUTO's cheek.

                    AUTO
My father died.

          JUDE kisses AUTO's neck.

                    AUTO
I stopped reading

JUDE kisses AUTO's chest.

AUTO

ran away from home

JUDE kisses AUTO's belly.

AUTO

and became notorious for telling people
there was no need to be afraid of what they thought.
I was a chirpy little self-proclaimed prophet
sitting around smelling my own farts
waiting for visions. For unicorns.
For messages written in the sky.
I would have rented a mentor if it was possible.

JUDE

I think it is possible in Vancouver now.

> *For the first time*
> *AUTO laughs*
> *and initiates*
> *a very silly*
> *very boyish*
> *miniature wrestling match/grope:*
> *for a moment it is summer*
> *and they are twelve years old.*
> *This relaxes into a full embrace.*
> *AUTO stares*
> *directly*
> *into JUDE's eyes.*

AUTO

I haven't looked in a mirror in a long long time.

JUDE

I look all the time.
I like pores.

                              AUTO
Pores?

                              JUDE
Pores.
I think pores are neat.

                              AUTO
You are one crazy little bastard aren't you.

                              JUDE
Nuts.

                              AUTO
Yeah. Nuts.

            Smiles.
            A kiss.
            Silence.

                              AUTO
Ever been attacked?
Beaten? Badly?
Close to death?

                              JUDE
No.

                              AUTO
No.
No I didn't think so.
I was. Got jumped.
Crazy rabid Nazi.
Crazy rabid doberman.
Somewhere in the middle of some night.
Barely remember it.
Didn't fight back.
Assholes.

                              87

A kiss.
They rearrange themselves
in each others' arms.
Silence.

                    AUTO

Courage.
Does that mean anything to you?
I have no idea what it means.

                    JUDE

Follow the yellow brick road.

                    AUTO

I don't think so. Anyway —
hear it's not worth the trip these days.
Full of potholes and roadkill and tourists.

              Smiles.
              A kiss.

                    AUTO

You don't smoke do you?

                    JUDE

No.
Well —
just drugs.

                    AUTO

I just drink.
Enough for a small farming community
but I just drink.

              Smiles.
              A kiss.
              They rearrange themselves

in each others' arms and legs.
Something gets pinched in the process.

JUDE

Ow.

AUTO

Sorry.

JUDE

It's okay.

Position established.
Silence.

AUTO

It's nice being this uncomfortable with you.

JUDE

Mmhm.

Silence.

AUTO

There's a "murmur" in my head.
Reminds me of the relief I felt on the day of the rescue.
The day Lyle rescued me from —
I don't know.

Silence.

AUTO

I crashed. I had crashed.
I had crashed head first into — into myself.
And Lyle was there. Lyle "appeared."
People do appear at certain times.

Auto kisses Jude
gently on the forehead.

AUTO

That's one thing I forgot I still believe.

Silence.

AUTO

"Murmur."
Words take any definition they need
when you don't speak often.
"Murmur."

Jude kisses Auto.

JUDE

Where were you living?

AUTO

When?

JUDE

When Lyle came on the scene.

AUTO

Hmmm.
Barely living.

A smile.

AUTO

Montreal.
He had all the answers I needed.
But I couldn't give anything back.
I couldn't give anything anywhere
let alone back.

So I'm giving it back now
but I don't know what I'm giving back
and I don't know how — when to stop.
Maybe I have stopped.
Maybe I haven't started.
Maybe I —
how long have you been here?
Fuck.
This room runs on twisted time.
Do I sound like him?
I'm starting to sound like him.
I'll look like him soon.

> JUDE *pulls* AUTO *into a kiss.*
> *They neck. Then*
> AUTO *pulls away.*

AUTO

What the fuck am I doing?

> *Silence.*

> LYLE *enters from behind the partition.*
> AUTO *and* JUDE *don't see him.*

JUDE

What does Lyle want?

AUTO

How old are you?

JUDE

What does Lyle want?

AUTO

Want?

JUDE

What does Lyle really want?

AUTO

If I knew I'd give it to him.

LYLE waltzes across the room.

LYLE

Auto and Judy
up in a tree
k-i-s-s-i-n-g.
Well!
I'm actually sleeping.
Must be the company.
My dreams are morbid
but at least I'm sleeping. Now —
will you stay for supper Jude?
I'm roasting a duck.
With baked pears
and potatoes.
Did you know
that potatoes only grow at night?

An awkward silence.

LYLE

Do I prepare three servings? Oh! Four!
David might be by.
He said he'd phone first
but he might be by.
Does he know the new phone code?
Auto does he know it's changed to three rings?

AUTO

David is in Halifax with Veronica Lyle.
You haven't seen him in years.

AUTO moves to his table
and begins to roll cigarettes
and drink.

LYLE

You whore.
You little fucking prick you —

JUDE

We can't stay for supper Lyle.
We're invited to my friend's place for brunch.

AUTO looks to JUDE.
JUDE begins to get dressed.

JUDE

It'll go into the evening.
Their brunches always do.

LYLE

Pardon me?

JUDE

Auto and I are invited to Carrie and Rue's for brunch.
We've been putting them off for weeks.
We can't anymore. Actually —
Carrie is interested in some of Auto's work —
some of his paintings.

AUTO is staring at JUDE.

Silence.

LYLE

Well.
Well this. This is.
Well this is wonderful.
Auto why didn't you tell me?

Silence.

                    LYLE

Auto?

     Silence.

                    AUTO

I wanted it to be a surprise.

                    LYLE

It's.
It's it's it's just
well it's just like pulling teeth
even trying to get him to tell me
how he spent his day. Well. Hah! My my.
My my my we'll just —
well we'll just have to have an opening.
This is wonderful wonderful fabulous wonderful.
We'll have to have an opening.
But Auto remember
before you go —

                    JUDE

We'll get cat food.

                    LYLE

Good.
Good good.
That will be perfect. Hah!
An opening.
We'll put this town on its ear.
They loved Auto in Venice they —

                    AUTO

Rest Lyle.

                              LYLE
What? Yes. But I'm so excited.

                              AUTO
Lyle.

                              LYLE
Baby?

                              AUTO
Rest.

                              LYLE
Yes. Yes I'll rest it's —
it's rare but
sometimes faith pays off.

          LYLE exits behind the partition.
          Silence.

                              AUTO
How long were you in jail?

                              JUDE
Over night.

                              AUTO
Six hundred and forty-three times twelve minus forty-eight.

                              JUDE
Seven thousand six hundred and sixty-eight.

          Silence.

                              AUTO
Lyle was the painter.
I've never met Aunt Sig.
We've never been to Venice.

                              95

He's been threatening
to roast that duck
for five years now.

Blackout.

SCENE SEVEN

/late afternoon/

> *LYLE is sprawled on the chaise*
> *drinking sherry*
> *and flipping through*
> *a fashion magazine.*
> *JUDE sits in AUTO's chair*
> *his camera close at hand*
> *listening attentively to LYLE.*

LYLE

It was a brazen morning.
A very cool indulgent day.
Technically it was summer
but autumn hung in the air like a jealous mistress.
I was thirty-three maybe?
Gawd — are people still thirty-three?
At any rate
I had just completed an evening
that had lasted well over fifteen years.
Fifteen years
of late night drug-induced close calls.
Fifteen years of coasting — tempting fate.
Fifteen years
that finally allowed me to acknowledge
the love that dare not "belch" its own name.

A laugh
and more sherry.

I was never a boy.
I never experienced
the love of another boy as a boy
so as a result I was never a boy.
And I do love boys.
I'm hopelessly devoted to boys.
But I'm not exactly a boy am I?

> *A brief silence*
> *and then*
> LYLE *plucks the perfume sampler*
> *from the pages of the magazine*
> *and smells it.*

LYLE

It's citrusy — I like that.

> *Another sniff.*

But there's a floral overtone that will cling:
death at an intimate dinner party.

> LYLE *tosses the sampler*
> *and the magazine on the floor.*
> *He pours another sherry.*
> LYLE *stares at* JUDE.
> *Silence.*

LYLE

You're eager
but not embarrassingly keen.
Quite a gift —
being able to disguise your hunger.

                            JUDE

You think I'm evil?

                            LYLE

I think you're lovely.

                            JUDE

I like you too Lyle.

                            LYLE

I believe you Jude.

            Silence.
            LYLE downs his sherry
            and pours another.

                            LYLE

I awake in the rain that morning —
naked on a rooftop in the east end of town
with no recollection of how or why
and as I had no benzedrine to make the world go away
I got dressed
and descended the fire escape
into the bowels of the city.
Then I phoned friends for money.
I had acquired quite a few wealthy friends over the years
whose only means of entertainment — was me.
There was a time when I was paid
to go to parties and just — talk.
At any rate
I phoned them — all of them
and they
like fathers of future brides
dished out healthy dowries:
royalties for all my years of cocktail chatter.
Then I booked the train for the east coast.
I have no family

but the family I did have
was from the east coast.
I'm a Newfie dear —
just another old queen from the rock.
So I left. Bon Voyage.
With thousands of dollars — cash — in my pocket
leaving behind a few worldly possessions:
a remote and impossible love named Veronica
and our child David —
both a result of my brief foray into "normality."

Another sherry.

The train trip left me hollow.
Reminded me rudely
that I had seen too much too soon.
I am very much afraid for this world
of this world
and this world is very much afraid of me.
And my fear is valid.
I'm no novice.
I've put in time.
More time and energy than most.
And believe me —
the pension plan is shit.

> *He laughs*
> *downs his sherry*
> *and pours another.*

Quebec was beautiful:
a cool streak of near white.
And the New Brunswick sunset
burned a hole in the sky
like the map at the beginning of Bonanza.

A fond smile.

And Nova Scotia —
Cape Breton:
marble skies smooth and blue but gold and pink.
And the ocean —
like my first lost thought of love:
as a child — a boy in my swimming class
with hair the colour of something else
and an ass like a plum in his brown purple suit:
so distant and — very scary.

> *Silence.*
> LYLE *is lost.*
>
> JUDE *snaps his photograph.*
> LYLE *looks to* JUDE.

JUDE

Don't stop Lyle.

LYLE

Um. I um —

JUDE

Where did you get off the train?

LYLE

The train?
We got off the train in Amsterdam
and stayed there for —

JUDE

In Canada Lyle.
On the east coast —
where did you get off the train?

LYLE

Where's Auto?

JUDE

The library.
He went to the library.
He needed to be alone.
He'll be back soon.

LYLE

Is he getting food for the babies?

JUDE

Yes.
After the library.
Where did you get off the train Lyle?

Silence.

LYLE

Nova Scotia.
I stumbled off the train in Nova Scotia.
Obviously
this was around the time when they drove the last spike.

Smiles.

Then I boarded the ferry in North Sydney
for Newfoundland.
I wanted to go to the end.
My family was from the end.

He pours the last of his sherry.

I'm out.

JUDE

I'll get it.

LYLE

You're an angel. It's —

JUDE

I know.

*JUDE gets a bottle of sherry
from the cabinet.*

LYLE

I rolled all night
like an ancient fetus
in the belly of that ferry.

*JUDE pours sherry for LYLE
leaves the bottle
and returns to AUTO's chair.*

LYLE

How do I know you'll be good to him?

JUDE

So whatcha do in Newfoundland Lyle?
Fish? Ride a whale?

LYLE

I have come very close to riding a whale my dear boy
very close
but on this particular occasion
it was not whale riding weather.

*They smile.
LYLE downs his sherry
and pours another.*

I found myself in the Codroy Valley
on an old bridge
that my great grandfather had constructed years ago.
And on that day
on that bridge

well —
I suppose I saw a light.
And I heard — well —
there was no sound
but in viewing the light —
I heard something.
This glaring whiteness told me
in a surprisingly formal tone
that I was soon to find love
in the form of one much younger than myself.
Well —
Jesus Mary and Joseph and the little mule too
wasn't that the madness setting in.
I said to myself
out loud on that bridge
"remember this feeling — this is it —
this is the madness setting in."

JUDE

How long after that did you meet him?

> *Silence.*
> *LYLE stares at JUDE.*
> *Silence.*

LYLE

Am I talking out loud?
Or are you just watching me
and I think I'm talking out loud?
Am I talking out loud?

JUDE

How long after that did you meet him?

> *Silence.*

LYLE

One week later.
To the day —
almost to the hour.

LYLE downs his sherry.

I'm getting very tired.
The pounding is in my legs
and I'm getting one of my headaches.

JUDE

He told me you met in Montreal.

Silence.

LYLE

If I told you something else
you'd only tell me the truth anyway wouldn't you.

Silence.

LYLE

Please don't be mean to me.

JUDE

I'd never be mean to you Lyle.

LYLE

Where is he?

JUDE

The library.

LYLE

Honestly?

JUDE

Yes.

Silence.

LYLE

Do you have a family?

JUDE

Yes.

LYLE

Do they love you?

JUDE

Yes.
Yes I think they do.
I'm not sure.

LYLE

Do they meet your friends?

JUDE

They did.
I've been on my own for a while now.

LYLE

Auto has no family.
He was born under a cabbage leaf.

Smiles.
Another sherry.

I began to travel west immediately.
I intended to go directly to Vancouver
but I stopped in Montreal.
I stopped in Montreal —
for a walk.

Silence.

Why did you take my picture?

JUDE

You were beautiful.

LYLE

Don't lie to me.

JUDE

I don't lie.

LYLE

A camera can be a cruel thing my son.

JUDE

I treat it with respect.
It's full of secrets.

LYLE

Full of freaks.

JUDE

Full of freaks' secrets.

LYLE

And eloquent too. So —
you're an alien?
A little mutant pansy from another galaxy?
Well I haven't met a mutant yet
that I didn't find fascinating.

Smiles.
Another sherry.
Silence.

He was shivering
sweating hot with the clap
drinking scotch
in a wrinkle room in Montreal the day I met him.
It was raining outside
and his socks were so wet
he had them draped over the arm of his chair.
He was a peculiar sight. Smoldering.
Angry enough to be right about everything.
Initially I just wanted his body.
I never dreamed he could possibly think the way he looked.

A fond smile.

How was I to know he was an Orlando?
How was I to know he sailed too high for me?

Silence.

I turned inside out.
Say good-bye now I thought
and you will live knowing you only felt it set in.
Stay and —

Silence.

I stayed.

Silence.

How did he come to live with me?

JUDE smiles.

LYLE
Am I making this easier for you
or easier for me?

JUDE

How did he come to live with you?

LYLE

I asked him to.
I asked him to start over with me.
I knew exactly where he was.
That was his only attraction to me
though it was overwhelming.
He was far more fascinated with that fact than I.

> *Silence.*
> *Another sherry.*

It's a sad thing
when two people
merely out of desperation
begin to become so much alike. Hm.
I used to have answers.
Now all I have is —
information.
Fragments.
Fragments of lives.
Fragments of gods.
Harpies. Tricksters.
The past.

> *Silence.*

I used him.
I paraded him. I wore him.
I let him snap around my ankles like a Chihuahua.

> *A smile.*
> *Silence.*

You'll look good together.
You'll look cocky and arrogant together.

108

Together
you're capable of making thousands hate you.
Cherish that.
Cherish that power.

Silence.

God love you —
you've almost got me coherent here haven't you.

Smiles.
Silence.

Why am I like this?
I know everything so —
why am I like this?

> *JUDE moves to LYLE*
> *and embraces him. Then*
> *JUDE takes LYLE's face in his hands*
> *And LYLE is charmed.*

JUDE

I'm going to meet Auto.
Then we're going to get cat food.
Then we're coming back here.

LYLE

You won't be long?

JUDE

We won't be long.

LYLE

The keys.

JUDE

I have the keys.

LYLE

Does he have his pills?

JUDE

Yes.

LYLE

Is it October?

JUDE

November.

LYLE

There was a windy day in October.
A Winnie the Pooh day: a blustery day.
I think that's the day everything changed.

JUDE

I was down by the harbour that day.
There were crows everywhere.
It was a warm wind for October.

LYLE

Wasn't it remarkable?

JUDE

Yes.

Silence.

LYLE

Will it hurt when you take him away from me?

JUDE

No.

Blackout.

SCENE EIGHT

/evening/

A full moon is rising.
The room is damp with its light.

The soiled sheets are gone.
The room is tidy.
The door to the cat pen is open.

AUTO enters
with a large bag of cat food
closing the door behind him.

All still.

The calmness
the complacency of the room
is unsettling for him.
He crouches on the floor
clutching the bag of cat food.
A deep breath.

He notices the door to the cat pen.
He moves slowly to the pen.

LYLE enters from behind the partition.
AUTO doesn't see him.

LYLE has showered
and is clean shaven.

He is wearing
a perfectly ironed silk shirt:
deep blue with gold flecks
like a burst of lapis lazuli.

Baggy khaki-coloured drawstring pants
and a larger than small
gold hoop earring in his left ear.
He is barefoot.
There is a freshness about him —
a resigned calm.
He seems taller.

LYLE watches AUTO kneel
and peer into the pen.
Then
gently:

LYLE

Boo.

AUTO starts.
He turns to LYLE.
Silence.

AUTO

You're dressed.

LYLE

Does it look as foreign as it feels?

AUTO

You haven't —
you haven't dressed in years.

LYLE

You've been reading.
You haven't read in years.
Is it possible we're regressing?

Silence.

112

> AUTO

Are you going out?

> LYLE

Of course not.

> *Silence.*

> AUTO

I haven't seen that shirt before.

> LYLE

I've never worn it before.
David gave it to me —
centuries ago.

> *Referring to the earring.*

> LYLE

And you gave me this.

> AUTO

I thought it was lost.

> LYLE

It was.

> AUTO

Where did you find it?

> LYLE

In this shirt pocket.

> *Silence.*

> LYLE

What were you reading?

                                AUTO
Newspapers.
Old newspapers.

                                LYLE
Have I missed anything?

                                AUTO
More of the same.

                Silence.

                                AUTO
Where are the —

                                LYLE
I set them free.
They were sick. They were fighting.
No room to run.
Their muscles weren't developing.
Carmen-Miranda and Betsy-Ross were both blind
and Chubby-Puss had just eaten a litter.
They had to go.

                                AUTO
That's been happening for some time now Lyle.

                                LYLE
I suppose I wasn't aware of the severity of the situation.

                                AUTO
How do you feel?

                                LYLE
Light.
Numb.
Tingly.

                                114

Silence.
AUTO moves to his table.

LYLE

Don't sit there.

AUTO doesn't.

Silence.

AUTO

Do you know what's happening?

LYLE

These pants don't quite work do they.

AUTO

They look fine.
You look wonderful.

LYLE

The cut is all wrong
but they'll do.

AUTO

For what?

LYLE

I have a date with the moon.
She's just beginning her first full night.
And not a star in the sky.
Amazing how she pulls it off —
even without accessories.

AUTO

You're making me nervous.
Well —
more nervous than usual.

Don't keep him waiting.

Silence.

AUTO

Jesus Christ Lyle
you can't
do not
please don't make this easy for me.

LYLE

The sky is opening up.
Your demons have no power anymore.
They have no power
because they really aren't demons at all.
They're just a bunch of —
chorus girls.

Silence.

AUTO

You can't stay here alone.

LYLE

The sky is opening up baby:
people are telling their own secrets
before the chorus girls get a chance to tell.

AUTO

I need a fight Lyle.
I want a fight.
I deserve a fight.
Please.

Silence.

Lyle —
I'm leaving this place.
I'm leaving you.
I'm leaving you for a guy who saw me in a dream.
I don't even know his last name.
He lives in the east end
across from a bakery that has an Elvis bust in the window.
That's all I know but —
I know him.
I believe him.
And I criticized my sister
for marrying a guy
she met five days before the wedding.
As far as I know they're still together.
Lyle. I have a sister.
I have a fucking sister Lyle —
isn't that something you should know?
Her name is Diane.
She was a finalist
in the Miss Canada pageant
in nineteen-seventy-fucking-something.
Isn't that something you should know?
I was the fastest sprinter on my high school track team.
I had meningitis when I was six years old.
I hallucinated for days.
My mother had holy water flown in from Rome.
My first paying job was for twenty bucks
dancing naked
to Barbra Streisand singing "The Way We Were"
for my grade six English teacher "after" school.
Aren't these things you should know Lyle?

Silence.

You're getting dumped Lyle.
Right here. Now.

You're getting dumped
by someone who just might be crazier than you.

                    LYLE
Baby please don't flatter yourself —
it isn't becoming.

        Silence.

                    AUTO
Okay. So. Right. Fine. Uh huh. Okay. So —
what's with the Pat Boone impersonation Lyle?
did you get a stronger prescription? is that it? huh?
When do the dishes fly Lyle?
When do you start throwing dishes?

                    LYLE
I've thrown them all.
I'm dishesless.

        Silence.

                    AUTO
Who's going to pump you with sherry Lyle?
Who's going to force-feed you before you pass out?
Who's going to mash up the carrots?
Who's going to see
that those pigs who own this place
get their rent?
You going to play "special drawer" with them?
You —
we —
have got to find a place for you Lyle we —

                    LYLE
You were never meant to live in my little aquarium.

                        .

                    AUTO
This isn't a little aquarium Lyle.
It's a fucking dive in the middle of a goddamn slum
that's getting bigger every minute.

                    LYLE
Ah but it's home and there's no place like —

                    AUTO
Don't!

        Silence.

                    AUTO
I hate you right now.

        Silence.

You've been lying to me for years.
I've been lying to you for years.

                    LYLE
You've never lied to me Auto.
You've accommodated me.
You should be given the Order of Canada
for deciphering madness.

                    AUTO
Fuck! You!
I've lived under you
around you
and for you
fighting to survive
terrified to live
for half of my fucking life
and I've never managed to decipher a fucking thing!

Silence.

Silence.

Silence.

LYLE

I'm sorry.

AUTO

Don't be sorry.
Just tell me one thing:
what did you save me from?
You could have been anyone.
I was completely open.
Anything could have been truth that day —
how many years ago?
Why did you want me?
Why did you take me?
What did you save me from? Myself?

Silence.

LYLE

I have no answer.
I have a clever one if you'd like.
But I have no real answer. I —
I recognized something in you I —

AUTO

Really? What?

Silence.

That's what I was running from:
being "recognized" as "something"
that was only real

if I promised to keep my mouth shut later.
I loved as a boy Lyle.
That was never a problem — at first.
I did. Love. As a boy.
Recklessly
one-sided and physical
but I DID love as a boy.
I sucked cock like a garbarator
and fell all over love Lyle
and finally the bullshit got to be too much.
Because in their eyes
ultimately
I was just a faggot.
In those boys' eyes
who pretended they were asleep
in those boys' eyes
who pretended they were too drunk
in those boys' eyes
who were just trying something NEW
in those boys' girlfriends' eyes
in those boys' wives' eyes
I was just a faggot.
A busy faggot
but just a faggot just the same.
Are you listening to me I am talking are you listening to me?!

LYLE

Yes.

Silence.

AUTO

Silence is hard work Lyle.
Filtering
all the voices in my head
into one
one that I could communicate with.

One that could keep me company.
I'm asleep when I'm awake.
I'm awake when I'm asleep.
Instead of living on the outside
I chose the inside. The other side.
And you saw this.
You saw all of this happening and you knew.
So why? Please —
why did you just watch?
What did you save me from?

Silence.

I'm not taking anything with me.

LYLE

You'll take this.

> *LYLE goes to the chaise*
> *and removes an overstuffed envelope*
> *and a small red book*
> *from its lining.*

AUTO

Blood money?

LYLE

Royalties.
And my address book.
There's a legend at the front.
Don't bother contacting the names
with the little dagger insignia beside them.

AUTO

Lyle.

122

LYLE

One more thing.
Avoid martyrdom.
And polyester.
Especially polyester.
No matter what those crazed queens tell you
about how brilliantly it takes colour —
avoid it.
As for martyrdom —
if you really crave that state
as do I: wallow.
I've always wanted to be a martyr.
Ever since I was a little girl.
Either that or a beautician.

Silence.
Smiles.

AUTO

You crazy old cocksucker.
You're a crazy old cocksucker Lyle.
You are one crazy old cocksucker.

LYLE smiles radiantly.

LYLE

Thank you.

All still.

LYLE opens his arms
and for the first time ever
they hug.

A whale call is heard.
AUTO starts.

LYLE

Don't keep him waiting.

Another whale call.

AUTO

What?
what was — what is that?

LYLE

Go.

AUTO

What?

Another whale call.
LYLE gives the envelope
and address book to AUTO.

LYLE

Go now.

Whale calls.

AUTO

Lyle?

LYLE

Go.
Now.

Whale calls.
LYLE guides AUTO to the door.

AUTO

Your eyes.
Your eyes are —

LYLE

Sh.

Whale calls.
LYLE opens the door.

AUTO

Lyle?

LYLE places his palms
fingers spread
over AUTO's face
and runs his fingers
the length of AUTO's face and neck.
AUTO is still.

LYLE

We are only here for a moment.

LYLE guides AUTO
gently through the door.

LYLE closes the door.
LYLE locks the door.

Whale calls: stronger.
An enormous thud against the wall.

LYLE's "waddle"
has practically disappeared.
He almost prowls
slices through the room.

An enormous thud against the wall.
The whale calls are constant now.

LYLE examines favourite knick-knacks

125

A thud.

LYLE arrives at AUTO's chair
and tucks it in place
under the table.

A chorus of whales.
Another thud.

LYLE moves to the chaise
sits
and pours a sherry.

Furniture slides.
The pen collapses.
The plaster on the walls
begins to crack.

The lights fade into lapis blue
And emerald green: flashes
fragments of light
like that created
when too much pressure
is applied to closed eyelids.

LYLE spreads out confidently
regally
on the chaise.

Another thud.
Another thud.
Another thud.

As water begins to leak
from cracks in the walls
LYLE toasts the world
defiantly with a smile.

The lights plunge into darkness.
Rushing water is heard.
The whale calls fade.

"Something Stupid"
sung by Frank and Nancy Sinatra plays.

THE BEGINNING